For Saskia
M.W.

First U.S. paperback edition 2002

The Library of Congress has cataloged the hardcover edition as follows:

Waddell, Martin.
Good job, Little Bear / Martin Waddell ;
illustrated by Barbara Firth. — 1st U.S. ed.
p.   cm.
Summary: Little Bear does a good job of climbing rocks, bouncing on a tree branch,
and crossing a stream, but Big Bear is always there to lend a helping hand when needed.
ISBN 0-7636-0736-3 (hardcover)
[1. Bears—Fiction. 2. Helpfulness—Fiction. 3. Self-reliance—Fiction.]
I. Firth, Barbara, ill. II. Title.
PZ7.W1137Gm   1999
[E]—dc21   98-23598

ISBN 0-7636-1709-1 (paperback)

4 6 8 10 9 7 5 3

Printed in Hong Kong

This book was typeset in Monotype Columbus.
The illustrations were done in pencil and watercolor.

Candlewick Press
2067 Massachusetts Avenue
Cambridge, Massachusetts 02140

visit us at www.candlewick.com

GOOD JOB, LITTLE BEAR

Martin Waddell

illustrated by Barbara Firth

CANDLEWICK PRESS
CAMBRIDGE, MASSACHUSETTS

Once there were two bears,

Big Bear and Little Bear.

Big Bear is the big bear

and Little Bear is the little bear.

One day, Little Bear wanted

to go exploring.

Little Bear led the way.

Little Bear found Bear Rock.

"Look at me!" Little Bear said.

"Where are you, Little Bear?" asked Big Bear.

"I'm exploring Bear Rock,"

Little Bear said. "Watch me climb."

"Good job, Little Bear,"

said Big Bear.

"I need you now, Big Bear,"

Little Bear shouted. "I'm jumping."

"I'm here, Little Bear," said Big Bear.

Little Bear jumped off Bear Rock

into the arms of Big Bear.

"I'm off exploring again!"

Little Bear said, and he ran

on in front of Big Bear.

Little Bear found

the old bendy tree.

"Look at me!" Little Bear said.

"I'm bouncing about

on the old bendy tree!"

Little Bear bounced on the branch.

"Watch me bounce higher,

Big Bear!" Little Bear said.

"Good job, Little Bear," said Big Bear.

"Are you ready, Big Bear?"

Little Bear called to Big Bear.

Little Bear bounced

higher and higher,

and he bounced

off the branch . . .

right into the arms of Big Bear.

"You caught me again!" Little Bear said.

"Good job, Little Bear," said Big Bear.

"I'm going exploring some more!"

Little Bear said.

Little Bear found the stream near the shady place.

"I'm going over the stream," Little Bear said.

"Look at me, Big Bear. Look at me crossing

the stream by myself."

"Good job, Little Bear,"

said Big Bear.

Little Bear hopped from one stone to another.

"I'm the best hopper there is!" Little Bear said.

Little Bear hopped again,

and again.

"Take care, Little Bear," said Big Bear.

"I am taking care," Little Bear said.

"Little Bear . . . !"

called Big Bear . . .

sploosh

"Help me, Big Bear,"
Little Bear cried.

Big Bear waded in, and he pulled

Little Bear out of the water.

"Don't cry, Little Bear," Big Bear said.

"We'll soon have you dry."

He hugged Little Bear.

"Let's go exploring some more,

Little Bear," said Big Bear.

"Exploring where?" Little Bear asked.

"On the far side of the stream," said Big Bear.

"Take care, Big Bear, you might fall

in like me," Little Bear said.

"Not if you show me the stone

where you slipped," said Big Bear.

"It was this stone," Little Bear said.

"Good job, Little Bear!"

said Big Bear.

Big Bear and Little Bear explored
their way home through the woods,
all the way back to the Bear Cave.

Big Bear and Little Bear settled down,

cozy and warm in the Bear Chair.

"Were you scared, Little Bear?" asked Big Bear.

"Were you scared when you fell in the water?"

"I knew you'd be there," Little Bear said.

"That's right, Little Bear," said Big Bear.

"I'll be there when

   you need me . . .

. . . always."